YOU ARE AN
OVERCOMER
PART 1

Journeying through Life on Purpose

by Don Scott

Publisher
Don E Publishing
www.donscottpublishing.com

First Edition
ISBN-13: 978-1-7397323-0-1- E-book
ISBN-13: 978-1-7397323-1-8 - Paperback

Publishing Consultants
Vike Springs Publishing Ltd.
www.vikesprings.com

Printed in the
United Kingdom and United States of America

For bookings and speaking engagements, contact us:
don.e.scott84@gmail.com

Don's books are available at special discounts when purchased in bulk for promotions or as donations for educational and training purposes.

LIMIT OF LIABILITY/ DISCLAIMER OF WARRANTY

Neither the publisher nor the author shall be liable for damages arising from actions undertaken based on information provided in this book. The fact that an organisation or website is referred to in this work as a citation and/or a potential source of further information does not mean that the author or the publisher endorses the information that the organisation or website may provide or recommendations it may make. Due to the ever-changing information from the web, Internet websites and URLs listed in this work may have changed or been removed. All trademarks or names referenced in this book are the property of their respective owners, and the publisher and author are not associated with any product or vendor mentioned.

DEDICATION

This book is dedicated to my family, mentors, and friends, present, past and future. In particular, special thanks to my wife, my mum, and my sister. A special dedication to the life and legacy of my friend Kimesha.

ACKNOWLEDGEMENTS

All the glory, honour, and praise belong to God Almighty. A massive vote of thanks to my publisher, Vike Springs Publishing, the team and their CEO and founder, Victor Kwegyir. I also want to thank all the people who have helped bring this dream to fruition, as well as those who have supported me with the launch and promotion of this book. Last but not least, YOU the reader, you didn't have to purchase, but you did. I am because you are. Love, light, and peace.

TABLE OF CONTENTS

INTRODUCTION.. viii

Chapter 1 - The Foundation 1

Chapter 2 - The Education 5

Chapter 3 - The Frenemies... 9

Chapter 4 - The Promise 13

Chapter 5 - Liberia 18

Chapter 6 - Fulfilling his Potential (God answers prayer)...............21

Chapter 7 - The Triple Anointing (Junior's thoughts).....................25

 Chapter 8 - David's Three Anointings (Junior's thoughts)............32

Chapter 9 – Practicalities (Junior's thoughts) 39

Conclusion 43

Note to Reader..45

INTRODUCTION

I have always wanted to write a book and share this story. My wish is to inspire people to aspire to greatness. It is my intention that as you read this book, you will not only enjoy reading but also learn something new. In addition, I want you to think of the various negative stereotypes about people who are at a disadvantage because of their skin colour, heritage, and social class, and how you can use this book's information to overcome your challenges peacefully. I would love you to also consider the goodness of God that is chasing us down in every situation

The lessons and thoughts in this book are greatly enhanced by reading alongside the workbook. I strongly encourage you to read both simultaneously. Finally, I want you to be able to shout: I AM AN OVERCOMER!! But, first, take a deep breath...

CHAPTER 1 - THE FOUNDATION

Life offers us many opportunities - some disguised as challenges with lots of lessons to learn if we choose to.

To understand how God can help someone overcome in life, we need to understand the foundation of their story.

Junior came from Jamaica as a 5-year-old to the UK, in a single-parent family. Junior did not know his dad or family on his dad's side, and his mum was his only family for over ten years. He was entirely dependent on his mum, and she was integral in building his early value system of hard work and nurturing him in doing the right things. Always a God-fearing woman, and even more so over time. She was and still is a prayer warrior and very loving woman and mother and did her best, to support Junior, but made it very clear that he had to go to university and she was very strict.

"You must have a degree so that you can make something of yourself in the future," she would always say as she emphasised why he needed to go to university. Her gaze remained solemn and fixed on Junior as she said these words. Her intense stare always made him look away while nodding in agreement, but he always left her satisfied by simply nodding in agreement.

Church at that time played a small role in Junior's life, and he always enjoyed going to church. In addition, his mum had an unusual gift of discernment. Various experiences, including spiritual battles, made Junior keen to know more, but these experiences would also scare him. He remembers numerous nights waking up to his mum praying. His family was heavily involved in church activities. His Uncle was a Pastor of 2 churches and the national administrator for his denomination. Over time most of his uncles and aunts on his mum's side would be saved, giving their life to God and followed on from Junior's maternal grandmother, who was also heavily involved in church activities. She was a wonderful woman of God who would spend a lot of time talking and singing about her Saviour to everyone that came to her house, whether saved or unsaved, family or not. She raised her six children primarily by herself as her husband died from a medical complication when he was quite young, and she never remarried. She devoted her life tirelessly to her family and raising six children by herself was no easy task.

She always told long and enticing stories about her life experiences. Despite having heard these stories many times before, Junior eagerly listened to her stories about how she came to the UK and experienced racism and a complete change of climate. She also narrated how she stayed for a few years and, eventually, tired of the continuous racial abuse, went back home to Jamaica. Although Junior grew up in a different country, spending time with her whenever she visited the UK or when he visited Jamaica made him very happy. She was an inspiration to him.

Junior's mum was born in the UK but grew up in Jamaica and wanted to return to the UK for greater opportunities for herself and Junior. Junior didn't realise he had struggled with moving to the UK from Jamaica until much later. Still, there were key signs, including that he had become more introverted and even forgot obvious things, like cycling. Knowing he had a brother and sister on his father's side, he was content being an only child to his mum, but Junior yearned for a sibling as he often felt lonely and he prayed at some point that he would meet his father's side of the family. His mother remarried and Junior was delighted to see her with her new husband, who made her so happy. He'd never forget the moment when he was eight when his mother and step-dad announced with tears in their eyes that he would soon become a big brother. Junior was ecstatic as he anticipated the baby's arrival, but his hopes were dashed when his mum had a miscarriage. Junior was sad and confused at the same time as the idea of a miscarriage sounded new and very confusing to him.

Junior's sister, Shelly, was born two years later. Junior was there to greet her and was overjoyed when his mother lovingly placed Shelly in his arms, cautioning him not to drop her.

Unfortunately, just when everything was going well, their happiness was cut short as his mother and step-dad split up. Although, Junior would still see his step-dad from time to time. Junior's mother was back to being a single parent and suppressed her sadness by resolving to face whatever life threw at her. Her determination, tenacity, and ability to adapt and change careers and family challenges were always something Junior struggled to understand. It was only by the grace of God she could endure these life battles. Junior's mum was an inspiration to him.

After the divorce, they moved to an estate that started as friendly and safe, but it became more and more crime-ridden as time progressed. The crime came from younger kids Junior did not know well, but drugs, violence, and crime became the norm over time. People were robbed and shot a few feet from their front door. Even though Junior knew all the main protagonists with time, he never ran with those crews. He wanted something better for himself and, because of his faith and that of his mother's, he knew it was possible. In addition, his mother's gift of discernment and her imperative that he get a good education scared him from going off the rails. Key scriptures Junior learnt at Sunday school always resonated with him, like:

Philippians 4:13 — 'I can do all things through Christ that strengthens me.' Proverbs 3:6 — 'Lean not unto your own understanding, but in all thy ways acknowledge him, and he shall direct your paths.'

CHAPTER 2 - THE EDUCATION

Junior was an excellent primary school student and very good at English. He and Daniel, a fellow schoolmate, always tried to outshine each other at the top of the class, but his main rival for the top of the class ended up going to Oxford. Junior thoroughly enjoyed primary school, even scoring well in his SATS. Towards the end of his primary school career, his family moved, and he had to commute every day.

However, he started secondary school at a school he did not want to go to. The school had approximately 36% of pupils receiving A-C in English and Maths, which was well below the national average. Junior struggled in his academics and making friends due to his home and environmental circumstances. However, Junior persevered, and the opportunities were awarded. He excelled in his year 9 SATS, obtaining a Level 6 in Maths and Science and a Level 8 in English. The national average was Level 4 and 5 in all subjects. Ultimately, Junior left the Secondary School with 3 A*s, 4 As, 1 B, and 1 C. Perseverance stopped him from becoming a statistic. By the end of secondary school, he had many friends and even had study evenings at his house to support them through their GCSEs.

During Junior's school years, his aunt, Eve, became critically sick. The doctors initially presumed it was an unknown disease but later diagnosed muscular dystrophy. The illness left her bed-bound creating difficulties as she had two young daughters and her husband, unfortunately, was no longer on the scene. The only family members she had in the UK were Junior, his mum, and his sister.

The illness meant that Eve and her two daughters moved in with Junior and his mum. Junior was 13, while his sister and 2 cousins were 2, 3, and 7. There simply wasn't enough space to accommodate them all, but they had to endure and manage. Junior's mum was at university and also working part-time. The situation was challenging and exceptionally stressful. Junior had to assist his mum with childcare, shopping, and other activities, making him responsible for many things at a very tender age. At that very young age, he knew how to pay bills, go shopping, and even started learning how to cook.

Junior also had to pick up at least one of the kids from the childminder after school or around his mother's schedule. The stress on Junior's mum was becoming too much that she was forced to request her nieces' father take responsibility for his children. This led to arguments with him as he didn't feel he could take on that responsibility. He preferred to continue living his best life, partying and drinking with friends. He claimed he was not in the right frame of mind to babysit. However, it had to be done as things became progressively worse. Most times, they didn't have enough to eat and sometimes only ate a meagre meal once a day to be able to eat the following day.

At this stage, the youngest niece went to her dad but ended up in Foster care after some time. Whilst she was in Foster care - Junior, his mum, and sister visited her frequently. Junior also had to take his other cousin back and forth from her dad's to her mum's on many occasions by taking the tube to Elephant & Castle from Leytonstone. He would often sleep during these journeys because he hardly ever had the time to rest.

Eventually, Junior's aunty, Eve, moved back to her home and became less bed-bound with the help of medical professionals, family, and friends, particularly Junior's grandmother. Even then, Junior still had to assist her, helping her cook, clean, shop, pay bills, etc.

By this time, Junior had forgotten how to socialise and have fun as his life had become exceptionally dull and stressful. He knew that things could not afford to remain the way they were, so he was always busy working and looking for ways to make their life situation better. Every time he even considered dropping out of school, he remembered what his mum always said to him, "You must have a degree so that you can make something of yourself in the future." In many ways, he wanted to be doing the same thing as his friends, playing sports and games, hanging out with friends, and socialising, but he just couldn't. His cousin from Jamaica came to live with them and helped Junior to be more social.

This also occurred around the same time Junior went through drama with his frenemies at school, making him feel very low. In hindsight, maybe this level of responsibility was helpful. It meant that Junior had a relatively easy transition into adulthood. It also meant he had less time to get into trouble with some of his more wayward friends. Although Junior felt in Lo-debar in many ways, he and his family could still move past that period. Whilst his aunty was not healed completely, things did become better.

As a result of all he had been through, Junior learnt to multitask, which also helped him when he started working with entrepreneurs who wanted his skills in web design, accounts, or digital marketing. He could manage many responsibilities and understood the mechanics of income and expenses pretty well by this stage.

We thank God that Junior had the strength and tenacity to move past this traumatic part of his life, drawing him closer to God and accepting Christ as his personal saviour and was baptised.

Junior's school wasn't the greatest, but he persevered and went to 6th form college, where he studied Economics, English Language, and Sociology. His 6th form college was a good college, and Junior was awarded an A and 2 B's in his A levels. After college, Junior attended Brunel University with a bursary from his 6th form college. The interview for the bursary was an interesting situation. It was held in a room full of older folks and councillors from the local council, seated at a very long table as though they were about to partake in a royal dinner. The selection committee was not very diverse, and Junior was concerned that he might not get the bursary, but he got it as God willed it.

Deuteronomy 28:13-13 — "And the Lord shall make thee the head, and not the tail; and thou shalt be above only, and thou shalt not be beneath; if that thou hearkens unto the commandments of the Lord thy God, which I command thee this day, to observe and to do them…"

CHAPTER 3 - THE FRENEMIES

Junior had many friends or, more likely, acquaintances growing up, and in secondary school. He was naive and thought that many of his friends would remain his friends forever. However, one particular person pretended to be his friend but publicly embarrassed him. It made no sense to Junior, so, as a more grounded and mature child, he chose to walk away from the situation instead of fighting.

This event started a long-running rivalry between two groups of teenagers, and whilst it never led to direct beef, the ongoing cold war could not be ignored. It led to embarrassment and anger on Junior's part and further alienation from people and, to some extent, fear. Junior's mother noticed the change in Junior's behaviour and personality, but he tried to assuage her concerns claiming it was nothing serious.

The cold war continued to brew, with both groups gaining friends and weapons. Junior also hung out with several people who pretended to be friendly. They even tried to kidnap Junior just to rob him at one point. Junior complied, to a point, and then ran away. However, it taught him that street life was not for him and that he had a future that others didn't. So, he removed himself from these frenemies, and consequently, the cold war dissipated as several on both sides were arrested. It was a highly challenging time for Junior, but he focused on:

Psalm 46 — 'God is our refuge and strength, a very present help in trouble.'

On another occasion, Junior went to Jamaica with his family. At the time, he was recovering from a long-term sickness.

Whilst there, a family friend asked if Junior could deliver a gift to his friend when they returned to the UK. The gift seemed innocuous but odd at the same time, as it was pretty clear that such a gift could be bought in the UK. Junior was suspicious, but since he was unwell at the time, he didn't argue. So Junior and his family took the gift, and the Lord gave them a message of deliverance. Miraculously, the vase they put the gift in went through customs quickly due to Junior's sickness. He was treated as a disabled person, so he was given a few special exceptions, aiding the quick release of their belongings.

Once landed and at home, this mysterious friend was calling non-stop for his gift, making Junior and his mum even more suspicious that they disassembled the gift. Let's just say that they would never have taken that gift had known better. If God had not intervened by paving a smooth path for them during the customs process, Junior and his family would have been locked up for a serious crime. Finally, a guy was sent to pick up the package releasing them of the burden.

The enemy will often come in a friendly way as though they are offering you something of relevance, but deep down, they are just there for their selfish desires or, even worst, harm you. Not every relationship is beneficial to you, and the faster one realises it, the better. God loves you too much. Remember:

1 Peter 5:8 — "Be sober, be vigilant; because your adversary the devil, as a roaring lion, walketh about, seeking whom he may devour."

As the psalmist says in Psalm 81:14 - "I would quickly subdue their enemies, and turn My hand against their adversaries."

After all that drama, Junior went to Brunel University, where he studied Business and Management for 4 years. For the 1st time in his academic career, he experienced academic failure. Not having family or social pressure, he felt relaxed and even tried to revitalise his social life, but unknowingly, he was losing sight of his primary focus, which was getting a good degree. However, after seeing his grades, he had to sit up. The loss of focus made him meditate on his mum and his purpose for attending university, which was enough for him to re-focus from the excitement of being at university that distracted him. He came back in the final year, getting a host of firsts in his subjects. He even went on to obtain another bursary.

"The Lord is angry for a night, but his favour lasts a lifetime; weeping may endure for a night, but joy cometh in the morning"— Psalm 30:5.

Junior has always enjoyed studying. When he left university with a degree, he went on to take various courses as he struggled to establish himself as someone of relevance to society. It was never crystal clear to him what he wanted to do, so he tried the company where he had previously gained some work experience, but they could only offer him temporary employment on the other side of London. So, he decided to stick it out and re-apply for graduate jobs he had previously not been successful in. This decision led him to attend new courses in the interim - digital marketing, web design, and teaching, all with the aim of having a career in these fields. However, he continuously underwent several disappointments from companies, friends, and even potential investors in the tech field. He made numerous plans and wrote several proposals to various firms to make his dreams of being successful come true. Still, it didn't happen, and it was an incredibly frustrating, depressing, and annoying time in Junior's life. Particularly, as all his friends were getting the jobs and careers they wanted, Junior was desperate for a breakthrough.

CHAPTER 4 - THE PROMISE

Junior struggled to find work after he finished university. He applied to various graduate jobs, but they were all abortive. He woke up at 5 am with a stomach ache one morning and thinking he was merely hungry. He had a cup of tea, but the pain continued. He continued in pain for about an hour and eventually took some painkillers, but the pain persisted, so he decided to wake up his mum. Being a prayerful woman, his mum laid her hands on Junior's stomach and prayed, but by merely laying her hands on his stomach, Junior started crying because the pain was so severe. His mum called a friend to take Junior to the hospital. At this point, the pain was so severe that Junior became even more uncomfortable and even vomited a few times. A few minutes later, Junior's mum managed to get him dressed, and she and her friend helped him to the car. The drive to the hospital was 5 minutes, and Junior's mum prayed even more on their way to the hospital. Junior grew weaker, even vomiting in the car.

Junior was immediately rushed into A and E, where the doctors examined his condition. Their initial prognosis was appendicitis, but they were sceptical as the pain wasn't coming from the correct area. So, they administered very strong painkillers, and the excruciating pain subsided a few minutes later. Junior was a lot more stable at this point that the doctor in charge even contemplated discharging him, but Junior's mum insisted he spend the night at the hospital for observation.

After a while, the pain returned, and this time even worse. The doctors were confused and suggested surgery to remove his appendix. The surgery would also enable them to carry out further examination and tests on Junior to ascertain the cause of the pain. In the midst of all his pain and the doctor's confusion, Junior was highly concerned, yet, he remained calm.

The time for the surgery came, and Junior was wheeled into the operating room, the anaesthesiologist administered the drug through an IV, and a few seconds later, Junior fell asleep. Junior's mum prayed fervently at the reception during the operation.

Junior woke up about an hour after the surgery and noticed the tubes and wires inserted into his mouth, nose, and the drip attached to his hand. He also noticed the scar on his stomach from the surgery. He was a bit confused as he believed that the operation was only an appendix removal, so why were all these tubes attached to him. He needed answers, but he was too sleepy and weak to keep his eyes open, and, before he knew it, he fell asleep again.

Junior woke up about 2 hours later, but, this time, the first thing he saw was his mum sitting next to him, sleeping. Looking around, he saw a nurse ensuring that he was stable. His mum, sensing that Junior was awake, woke up and immediately hugged him when Junior reached for her hand. He could see the tiredness in her eyes. Junior tried to seek answers as to why tubes were inserted into his mouth, but he could barely speak. The nurse later explained to him that he had a burst duodenal ulcer. An ulcer had burst in his stomach, and half-digested food and acid were slowly seeping into his abdomen, poisoning him.

Junior spent 10 days in the hospital and had to have physio to walk again. After 10 days, he could eat normally. There were a few setbacks when his stomach would not comply, but he made it through. Junior was also advised to stay home and rest since he had to heal from the appendix, ulcer operation and the pain. So, he took 3 months off work. This period wasn't really the best time for him to be off work, as he was only working part-time. Junior was only 23, and he'd see his friends doing well in their careers, buying cars, getting good jobs, and moving on with their lives, while he felt he wasn't progressing at all. But, as we all know, God's time is always the best.

One of the things that helped Junior through this difficult time was a song titled, 'Your latter will be greater' by Israel Houghton. This song helped him understand that everything happening was for a reason, and God had a perfect plan for his life. He also watched inspiring and church-related programs on TV, which helped shape his perception of all that had happened in his life. He also had wonderful friends and family who assisted him, were there for him, prayed with him, and helped Junior remain steadfast in the Lord. This period drew him closer to God, and he even wrote a few incredible gospel songs. After the 3 months, Junior returned to work even more diligently than ever. He made sure to put the fear of God into his work, and just 3 months later, Junior miraculously got his healing. He went back to the hospital for a follow-up examination, and the doctors were shocked. They pointed out that it was as though he had never experienced any ulcer problems, and his stomach organ was as good as new. Little did Junior know that his breakthrough was on its way.

"In their hearts humans plan their course, but the Lord establishes their steps." -Proverbs 16:9

Junior's break finally came when he applied at a top 10 firm for the second time. He originally applied for part of the Internal Auditing team. He got an interview with the firm and passed with flying colours. But, after some time, he was told there were no vacancies as all the places on the auditing team were taken. However, whilst waiting for an opportunity or vacancy, he was asked to come to a Partner practice interview. After the interview, he had to apply for a different position in consulting since the auditing team was still full. He also did an assessment test, which he equally passed with flying colours. When he arrived at the office, he was informed that the last spot was taken that morning. He was still at square zero.

Hebrews 10:36 — "For ye have need of patience, that, after ye have done the will of God, ye might receive the promise."

Junior was extremely frustrated. He was even more confused because he always passed these assessments but was always being turned down when it came to actually getting the job. But, he wouldn't give up, so he applied to another team. Junior decided to pick Compliance consulting as he had no desire to pursue audit or tax. He had done a total of 5 interviews just to get the job.

Rev 3: 8-9 — "However, when God opens a door, no man can shut it, and when God closes a door, no one can open."

Jeremiah 29:11 — "For I know the plans I have for you declares the Lord, plans to prosper you and not to harm you, plans to give you hope and a future."

Junior enjoyed the job but found many areas challenging. However, he was grateful for the opportunity, as the world was experiencing a financial crisis. Junior was surprised that he was the only black person in a client-facing role across various floors of people. However, this did not faze him. It meant that he had to understand a work culture he had never known before, but, as his experience in Liberia attested, it meant that Junior was competent in dealing with various cultures. While his team moved the department a year later, Junior decided to stay in consulting as he enjoyed the role.

CHAPTER 5 - LIBERIA

Junior had been at the Top 10 firm for a year when he was asked to go to Liberia go on a project to help analyse and build the controls for a large organisation. Junior had a sense of excitement but also of trepidation with this project. He wasn't very comfortable staying in Liberia at the time. He had many thoughts running through his mind but became calm after being assured his security and safety. He lived in a fancy hotel during his time there and had to check in at a specific time with the security firm in charge of his safety. These were a few of the processes put in place to ensure his safety.

Junior found Liberia fascinating, and even though he had only recently graduated, he excelled in the project and was treated as an expert. The contrast between poverty and abundance was startling. However, it was peaceful. Junior made several friends amongst the locals as they thought he looked like a local. He blended in so well that it felt like he had been staying there for longer and spiced up his social life as he would often have Wednesday football sessions with the client.

He also took the time to explore the history of the country and the nightlife of the surrounding cities. On one of these occasions, he visited several ancient archaeological sites, huge ruin sites preserved and in near perfect condition. He had other interesting adventures, like the Icelandic ash cloud event. The ash cloud was wreaking havoc with air travel across Europe. Junior had initially planned to go home to London that coming Friday, but, unfortunately, all flights were cancelled and suspended due to the ash cloud. Junior and his immediate boss were put on a standby flight for Saturday, but they got the confirmation too late. As a result, they had to fly home the following day, which happened to be Sunday.

Due to the nature of the journey and the flight trouble, they had to first fly to Rome when they were supposed to go to Milan. Arriving in Rome, Junior and his boss had to look for a way to get to Milan. The only fastest and possible way to get to Milan was by train, as there were no flights north of Rome. Luckily for them, Junior's boss had a little knowledge of Italian, and could communicate with a few of the locals, and they managed to get train tickets, escaping the long queue. As soon as they got on the train, they contacted their travel team to book a hotel in Milan.

When they got to Milan, they were informed that there wouldn't be a train going to Paris for several days, which meant they had to hang in Milan for a while. It was frustrating for Junior and his boss, as their schedules would have to be altered, and this didn't sit well with Junior's boss. So, they had to put in the extra effort to look for a possible midnight train to transport them to Paris. Fortunately, they found a midnight train going to Paris, but the price was excessively overpriced due to high demand. However, Junior and his boss just wanted to get to their destination as soon as possible, so they paid for the tickets.

After securing their tickets, Junior and his boss went to the hotel already booked by their team. They had to freshen up, eat, and then wait for midnight. Eventually, they got on the train, securing their overnight bunks.

Thankfully, it was summer as the train journeyed through several countries and they could enjoy the passing scenery in the morning. Finally, the train arrived in Paris midday the next day. Junior's boss could join a conference he wanted to attend, and Junior got home through Eurostar. Despite all the obstacles and delays, they met their various schedules and were on time. Thank God he made the crooked path straight. He went back to Liberia the following year, but this time, his visit was brief, peaceful, and a lot less stressful than the previous one, but that was the last time Junior visited Liberia.

The Wars: Court Threats

While Junior worked in Liberia, his reports were audited in the company unknowingly. As God remained faithful, Junior passed with flying colours. It meant that he received requests to attend court cases on various occasions, but he had no relevant information for the cases and so didn't attend. However, the prospect of going to court was daunting. Throughout Junior's career, he had to enforce rules and investigate companies. Litigation threatened Junior's career several times, which was always worrying as it is challenging to do a job and do the right thing with the fear of litigation.

However, Psalm 34:6 says "This poor man cried, and the Lord heard him and saved him out of all his troubles." Junior guessed these people also had a forgiving heart, and he thanked God for this mercy.

CHAPTER 6 - FULFILLING HIS POTENTIAL (GOD ANSWERS PRAYER)

Despite all the potential concerns, Junior excelled in his team, securing 2 major promotions in 4 years and not without opposition or other senior staff seeking to take advantage of his aptitude. Junior decided to expand his horizons and go abroad for more international experience. He went to the Netherlands, where he was sought after and even got a double promotion within 18 months. Junior was keen to give back to the community and, as a result, he became a trustee of a charity with the objective of raising career aspirations of those from disadvantaged backgrounds. Junior was the treasurer, and during his 5-year tenure, the charity was very successful. The charity supported government initiatives, and the income grew massively whilst Junior was there.

Junior had several girlfriends, but none too serious. He was focused on his career and his busy schedule did not permit the relationship to last very long. It was difficult to find someone to settle down with, as Junior had specific criteria. He thought sometimes he was being too specific, but he was keen to have a wife of the Proverbs 31 type, and not a woman who brought nothing to the table or was driven by money and status.

He thoroughly enjoyed the Netherlands, but he yearned for Michelle. He met Michelle through a mutual friend, Lisa. Lisa knew Junior from church for many years and wanted to hook him up with her friend, Michelle. However, Michelle did not live in London, so Junior would have to make many journeys to see Michelle and his other family and friends. Over time, they became very fond of each other, always losing track of time whenever they were together. He couldn't wait to tell her about his work abroad when he returned to the UK. He knew Michelle was special, and he planned to marry her in the near future.

Junior would constantly pray to meet his father's side of the family for many years, but over time other prayers became more urgent and necessary, and, eventually, he stopped praying for this. However, God did not forget. On a particular weekend, Junior was surprised when his Uncle called him from Jamaica and asked, "Do you want to speak to your Dad?" Junior was confused, immediately thinking it was some sort of joke? Junior thought about it for a little while. Could this be the chance to reconcile? Would his family like him? So many thoughts raced through his mind. Junior knew he had to accept the offer.

When Junior called his Dad, he was in New York, and it was difficult to hear him. However, Junior was happy to hear from his Father. Many questions raced through his mind. How did he find him? Why now? But, Junior went along with it. On top of his mind was getting in contact with his other siblings. Junior was able to exchange details with his father to contact his siblings. It was awkward at first when Junior and his siblings got in touch as if meeting someone out of the blue whom you never had or would never normally speak to. However, as time went on, the relationships grew stronger, and a bond slowly formed. He went to America to meet his family and had a great time. Junior and his sister, Anne's love of travel meant that they travelled together on more than one occasion.

One particularly interesting story was when they went to Australia for Junior's birthday. They decided to go out of the city and into the Blue Mountain area to look at the natural sites. They were the only 2 black people they could see for miles, but they enjoyed the trekking and were ready to go back to the hotel. However, they realised that they missed the last bus despite their best efforts, mainly because they broke away from the rest of the group. There they were, running up the hill and chasing this bus with no real way of knowing how they would get to their destination. Despair and exhaustion started to set in, and Junior and his sister decided to walk. As they were walking, a white van turned up out of nowhere, and a barefoot lady jumped out and asked if they wanted a ride. Junior said, "Thank you, Jesus," but his sister was a little bit more cautious. After much contemplation, they got in the van. Junior tried to engage in conversation and act normal, whilst his sister kept texting him, saying, "This is how people die!" Junior had faith and felt he could handle himself if things didn't go to plan. In the end, they managed to get to the station and get back to the hotel. Junior and his sister laughed at the situation afterwards, but at the time, they could already see the newspaper headlines: '2 Black people disappeared and found dead in a van'.

Junior thanked God for his faithfulness. God answers prayers. He also thanked Him for the father figures he was given when his father was not in his life. The Bible says:

Psalm 27:10 (NLT) "Even if my father and mother abandon me, the LORD will hold me close."

(NLT) 2 Corinthians 5: 17 "This means that anyone who belongs to Christ has become a new person. The old life is gone; a new life has begun.

18, "And all of this is a gift from God, who brought us back to himself through Christ. And God has given us this task of reconciling people to him.

19, "For God was in Christ, reconciling the world to himself, no longer counting people's sins against them. And he gave us this wonderful message of reconciliation.

20, "So we are Christ's ambassadors; God is making his appeal through us. We speak for Christ when we plead, "Come back to God."

Reflecting on Junior's tumultuous educational journey, this bible verse is only fitting: "The Lord is my strength and my shield. My heart trusts him. I was helped, my heart rejoiced, and I thanked him with my song." — Psalm 28:7 Psalm 37: 23 — "The steps of a good man are ordered by the Lord: and he delighteth in his way."

Proverbs 18: 22 — "Who so findeth a wife findeth a good thing and obtaineth favour of the LORD."

Junior could confidently say, like Solomon, that, "To everything there is a season, and a time to every purpose under the heaven." Ecclesiastes 3:1

CHAPTER 7 - THE TRIPLE ANOINTING (JUNIOR'S THOUGHTS)

Junior read extensively and remembered a passage from one of his local Elders on the triple anointing that he found interesting. He also heard a passage from a Bishop when he was visiting America. These words gave him a unique perspective on David's triple anointing from the Bible. One of Junior's friends gave him a book on the seasons of men, which he considered in more detail. Junior considered how it applied to various stages in life and wanted others to understand the message so that you don't have to stay where you are in spiritual, emotional, or mental states. Some relevant points are below.

"First anointing: Lepers anointing – Leviticus 14:14-18.

Lev 14:14 "The priest shall take some of the blood of the trespass offering, and the priest shall put it on the tip of the right ear of him who is to be cleansed, on the thumb of his right hand, and on the big toe of his right foot."

Lev 14:15 "And the priest shall take some of the log of oil, and pour it into the palm of his own left hand."

Lev 14:16 "Then the priest shall dip his right finger in the oil that is in his left hand, and shall sprinkle some of the oil with his finger seven times before the LORD."

Lev 14:17 "And of the rest of the oil in his hand, the priest shall put some on the tip of the right ear of him who is to be cleansed, on the thumb of his right hand, and on the big toe of his right foot, on the blood of the trespass offering."

Lev 14:18 "The rest of the oil that is in the priest's hand he shall put on the head of him who is to be cleansed. So the priest shall make atonement for him before the LORD."

Leviticus 14 outlines a series of procedures that the leper and priest must follow. These procedures had to be followed in the correct order for healing to occur.

First, the leper offered a lamb for a trespass offering Lev 14:13.

Lev 14:13 "Then he shall kill the lamb in the place where he kills the sin offering and the burnt offering, in a holy place; for as the sin offering is the priest's, so is the trespass offering. It is most holy."

The blood of the lamb was then applied to the right ear, the right thumb, and the big toe of the right foot.

After the blood was applied, the anointing oil was applied to the same spot on the ear, thumb, and toe, v.17 and v.25.

Ear = hearing

As sinners, we refused to hear God's commandments and continually break them.

As Christians, we listen to the voice of the Good Shepherd and keep His commandments (John 10:4, 5) to love and serve one another.

Thumb = service

Gal 5:13 "For you, brethren, have been called to liberty; only do not use liberty as an opportunity for the flesh, but through love serve one another."

Luke 10:30-37 – Example of the good Samaritan

As Christians "washed by the blood of the Lamb," we use our gifts to serve God and others.

We use our hands to heal and to help others.

Toe = walk

As unclean with the leprosy of sin, we walked in ways of rebellion, wickedness, and strife.

When the blood is applied, we renounce hidden works of darkness and immorality and walk in paths of righteousness and purity.

The story of leprosy symbolises the Holy Spirit's work in salvation when we are cleansed from our "spiritual leprosy" sin.

Just as leprosy moves into the physical body and destroys it, so sin moves in to destroy and kill the spirit.

In the Old Testament, there are two examples of leper healing: the story of Miriam and the story of Naaman.

It was not only the blood of the Lamb that cleansed the leper; it was also the anointing oil (symbol of the Holy Spirit) that restored him.

The Holy Spirit comes to empower our hearing, to empower us for service, and to empower us to walk uprightly.

So, leper anointing illustrates the work of the Holy Spirit in redeeming us to God for His pleasure.

Rev 5:9 "And they sang a new song, saying: You are worthy to take the scroll and to open its seals; for you were slain, and have redeemed us to God by Your blood out of every tribe and tongue and people and nation."

Second anointing: The Priestly Anointing - Exodus 29:29 and 30:30

Exodus 29:29 "And the holy garments of Aaron shall be his sons' after him, to be anointed in them and to be consecrated in them." This was for Aaron and his sons, the priests of the tribe of Levi.

Exodus 30:30 "And you shall anoint Aaron and his sons, and consecrate them, that they may minister to Me as priests."

The work of the God's Spirit in our life saves us from the guilt and penalty of sin, but also the Lord wants to save us from the power of sin, the habit, and the force of it.

The Spirit's work makes us holy, righteous, and express righteous deeds through service to others and the Lord. Cleansing.

The anointing comes into our lives to break all influence of sin upon us. The Holy Spirit breaks the power of cancelled sin.

Isaiah 10:27 - "... the yoke (of sin) shall be destroyed because of the anointing."

The priestly anointing is for holiness, to cause us to live right, produce righteous acts, and motivate righteous deeds.

Third anointing: The Kingly Anointing – 1 Samuel 10:1 and 16:13

1 Sam 10:1 "Then Samuel took a flask of oil and poured it on his head, and kissed him and said: Is it not because the LORD has anointed you commander over His inheritance?"

1 Sam 16:13 "Then Samuel took the horn of oil and anointed him in the midst of his brothers, and the Spirit of the LORD came upon David from that day forward. So Samuel arose and went to Ramah."

Thirdly, the anointing of a king is described in the Old Testament. A king's anointing was an anointing for power and authority. David was the only one recorded in scripture who was anointed three times. He had been anointed King, but his time had not yet come. He was anointed as King of Judah in Ziklag, taking on priestly garments. Finally, he was anointed King of Judah and Israel after Saul's death and reigned until his death.

It is the kingly anointing that Jesus spoke of to His disciples in Acts 1:8 "Ye shall receive power, after that the Holy Spirit comes upon you, and you shall be witnesses unto Me..." He wanted them to go out and preach the gospel with power.

It was never Jesus's intent that the gospel should be delivered "...in word only, but in demonstration of the Spirit and of power, that your faith should not stand in the wisdom of men, but in the power of God." I Corinthians 2:4-5

Jesus commissioned His disciples to go out and preach, heal the sick, and cast out devils. "...freely you have received, freely give." (Matthew 10:8).

He never expected the world to believe a gospel devoid of power.

He expected that "these signs shall follow them that believe. They would cast out devils, speak with other tongues, lay hands on the sick, and they would recover." (Mark 16:15 20).

Paul writes in Romans 15:19, "...from Jerusalem, and round about Illyricum, I have fully preached the gospel of Christ."

The Gentiles Paul preached to were made obedient not by word only but by "word and deed."

Acts 8:5-6 "Phillip went down to the city of Samaria and preached Christ unto them. The people with one accord gave heed unto those things which Phillip spake, hearing and seeing the miracles which he did."

The sick were healed. The demons were cast out, and there was great joy in that city."

CHAPTER 8 - DAVID'S THREE ANOINTINGS (JUNIOR'S THOUGHTS)

"There were three distinct anointing's in David's life.

David's First Anointing - Leper's Anointing

In 1 Samuel 16:13, we find David's first anointing. David was a young man at this time, but this was his call to be king. He was called, and the anointing was given to him.

1 Sam 16:13 "Then Samuel took the horn of oil and anointed him in the midst of his brothers, and the Spirit of the LORD came upon David from that day forward. So Samuel arose and went to Ramah."

It is worth noting that David's exploits didn't begin until the anointing. David didn't kill giants until after the anointing.

How many of us have gone out to do battle with giants without the anointing? The result is brokenness, confusion, burnout, etc.

1) After David's anointing as king, he came into an anointed ministry of music

1 Sam 16:23 "And so it was, whenever the spirit from God was upon Saul, that David would take a harp and play it with his hand. Then Saul would become refreshed and well, and the distressing spirit would depart from him."

His music caused the evil spirit to depart from Saul.

2) Another anointed ministry David moved into was becoming the armour-bearer of the king…

1 Sam 16:21 So David came to Saul and stood before him. And he loved him greatly, and he became his armour-bearer.

3) He received strength after that anointing in 1 Sam 17:34 35 "...there came a lion and a bear and took a lamb out of the flock. I went out after him and smote him... and slew him."

4) Later, we see him killing Goliath (1 Sam 17:49-51). Isn't this a bit strange for a teenage boy to possess such ability and courage? Well, you need to remember that he already had the anointing.

5) By chapter 18:7, we find the women of Israel singing, "...Saul has slain his thousands, and David his tens of thousands."

6) Now we come to the most dangerous part of the anointing; the applause of people.

How many people realise that you're on dangerous ground when people start applauding you? At least David learned to handle it. 1 Samuel 18:14 "David behave himself wisely in all his ways..."

David's Second Anointing - Priestly Anointing - The time of sanctification.

We want to look at this briefly. This anointing has been called the sign of David being chosen.

Matthew 20:16 "...many are called, but few are chosen."

1 Samuel 19:31 show many tests David passed through

Isaiah 48:10 "...I have chosen thee in the furnace of affliction."

This is where the Lord makes His choice. David passed through the furnace of affliction and became the chosen man of God.

King David passed the test; that's why he was not only called but he was also chosen.

When the anointing comes upon you, you will go through years of being checked by God.

Many of us fail the test and are never chosen during the "called" period under the kingly anointing.

We never go on to that second anointing. We become casualties because of pride or failure in particular areas.

But David passed the test.

In the event of David's second anointing, the Bible says in II Samuel 2:4, "the men of Judah came, and there they anointed David king over the house of Judah..."

On this occasion, David became the king that Samuel anointed him to be many years before. He began his reign in Judah. He was previously a king without a kingdom.

David was 30 years old when this anointing took place. (II Samuel 5:4 tells us this).

Probably 13-15 years have passed since Samuel anointed him, and those have been years of trials, being hunted like an animal by Saul, living in caves, gathering outcasts, the poor, those in trouble, and fugitives from the law.

They all fled to David. Only David could have led and controlled such a motley crew.

David's years of testing were part of God's preparation for him to take the throne for which he was anointed.

During this time, David also dealt with a divided kingdom, which made things difficult, but he persevered.

II Samuel 3:1 "there was a long war between the house of Saul and the house of David: but David waxed stronger and stronger, and the house of Saul waxed weaker and weaker."

At this stage of God's dealings in your life, you begin to rule and reign spiritually.

You start exercising the calling, the gift that God placed upon your life when you were first anointed.

Your enemies become subdued, and God starts giving you great triumph and victory. Notice how this happened in stages?

Many victories followed David's first anointing, then years of hardship and testing.

When David was anointed to the throne of the southern kingdom for the second time, a long war broke out between his house and the house of Saul.

Paul, the apostle, went through the same process. It was fourteen years before the prophets confirmed his ministry in the church of Antioch.

Now, we are ready for the third anointing.

David's Third Anointing - The Kingly Anointing

David's third anointing occurred on a particularly joyous occasion on his land's traditionally divided northern and southern kingdoms.

II Samuel 5 shows us the great blessing emanating from David's faithful service to God.

He was already king over Judah, which included the tribe of Benjamin, and now he also became king over Israel, the ten northern tribes (v.3).

On this occasion, he received his third anointing.

Not only were the northern and southern kingdoms united and David's enemies subdued but also a great event occurred on the third anointing.

In II Samuel 6:2-16, we find the story of David bringing the ark of God back to its resting place on Mt. Zion.

Keep in mind that the ark is symbolic of the glory of God.

1 Chronicles 16:37 and 25:1-7 record this event.

Psalm 134:1 "Come, bless the Lord, all ye servants of the Lord, who stand by night in the house of the Lord."

David had praise music blasting out 24 hours a day. The three stages of anointing may also be linked to Revelation 17:14.

This verse speaks of the Lamb of God, Jesus, triumphing over those who oppose Him, with the assistance of those "Called, Chosen, and Faithful."

These are the people who follow the Lord Jesus to victory over His foes.

Following David's third anointing, symbolising his faithfulness, came the complete subduing of all enemy kingdoms near Israel.

So, the Leper's Anointing is our call to salvation, Priestly Anointing is our call to service, and Kingly Anointing is our call to faithful obedience to the Lord.

Remember that failure happens in all these areas. David committed adultery, murder, and other sins after his third anointing.

When peace is at hand, we must maintain our guard."

CHAPTER 9 – PRACTICALITIES (JUNIOR'S THOUGHTS)

Numbers 22:18 "...I cannot go beyond the Word of the Lord my God, to do less or more."

Balaam's statement is one we need to take to heart. You cannot go beyond the anointing of the Lord your God and should not try to do less or more.

We have two significant problems in the church today.

The first problem comes from those anointed but not functioning in their anointing, doing less than they are anointed to do.

Paul wrote Timothy to "...stir up the gift..." (II Tim. 1:6)

The second problem is that we have people trying to do things they are not anointed to do; going beyond the anointing.

This is what happened to Saul. He extended himself beyond his gift.

He didn't have the priestly anointing. He tried to fulfil the office of a priest. He grew tired of waiting for Samuel, the priest, so he took over Samuel's duties with only a kingly anointing on his life.

David appeared to have received both a priestly and a kingly anointing. He was King-Priest, a foreshadow of the Messiah.[1]

---

1   Bill Burnett, written Nov 16, 2006, accessed 1 Jan 2022 The Three Anointings In The Bible Sermon by Bill Burnett, Leviticus 14:14-18 - SermonCentral.com

This occurs in the secular world, too. We could use the word capabilities instead of anointing. There will always be people capable but need to be encouraged to do something or stretch themselves as a leader or manager. There will also be those who attempt to act far beyond their abilities. Furthermore, some people have a lot of talent but lack the maturity to play a specific role during that season.

There are different seasons in the same way that we have different anointings. Solomon mentioned a season for everything in Ecclesiastes 3:3. Men have different seasons in their lives, such as the childish season, the cowboy season, the warrior season, the kingly season, and the sage or mentoring season[2]. There is similar for women. Other than the sage or mentoring season, the seasons and anointing interplay. A person's king season and anointing should ideally coincide in their lives over the area that God has given them. However, this isn't always the case.

Furthermore, the sage or mentoring season is not a change in anointing but rather the acceptance of a new role. In this case, for physical or other reasons, the King may decide to step back and allow another person to come through, after which they mentor or shepherd. This is what Paul was doing in I and II Timothy precisely: he poured out all of his knowledge to Timothy and reminded him always to study to show himself approved. It is noteworthy coming from someone who claimed to be a well-read student of the law and a Pharisee. Paul mentions in Acts being taught

---

2   Eldredge, J (2001), Wild at Heart: Discovering the Secret of a Man's Soul, Thomas Nelson/ John Eldredge publishing, New York, United States.

by Gamaliel and still being a student.

In God's Kingdom, there is no need for Kings to compete. We recall that Paul and Peter were apostles who disagreed, but this was acceptable because Paul was called to preach to the Gentiles and Peter to the Jews.

When the anointing of the Leper coincides with the Cowboy stage, we are saved from the punishment of sin. It is the most basic level of anointing and denotes that you are armed and dangerous to the Kingdom of Hell, but we are untrained, similar to the connotation of a cowboy.

Like the sons of Sceva, some Christians remain at this level of anointing and maturity. These Christians desire to cast out demons but lack maturity or anointing.

You do not need a title to be a priest; this anointing refers to being holy. The priestly anointing and warrior season are extremely important, but it is a stage where a person comes into their own and becomes a warrior to establish themselves. Many young people are here, and if not properly mentored, they become permanently frustrated because neither they nor their leaders see or articulate their potential.

Similarly, people can have a kingly anointing while still in a warrior maturity level, fighting against everyone and everything that is destructive to everyone. The key is to understand what season you are in and your anointing. What season or anointing are you currently in? Everyone must go through various maturation stages. There is nothing wrong with some people staying longer than others in certain seasons. You impact and are a blessing no matter what season or maturity level you are in. Below is a visual representation of seasons and anointing at a high level and in proposed progression through the anointing and seasons.

Anointing	Season
Leper	Cowboy
Priestly	Warrior
King	King
	Sage

Also, it doesn't mean you should overstay in a season; there can be a significant blessing in being in the sage or mentor stage, which many people avoid because they want to be in the King's season forever. Location is also an important aspect. God can bless you in a specific location because he has given you oversight of that area. Remember, Heaven and Earth will pass away, but God's word will live forever. It is critical to read, study, and comprehend the Word of God.

In all these things, Junior considered the following scriptures were authentic to him.

Job 23:10 — "But he knoweth the way that I take: when he hath tried me, I shall come forth as gold."

CONCLUSION

Solomon says in Ecclesiastes 12:13, "Let us hear the conclusion of the whole matter: Fear God, and keep his commandments: for this is the whole duty of man."

Junior can genuinely say that God is good and his mercies endureth forever. He can look back over his life and see the goodness of God was indeed chasing after him. Junior has many more stories to tell, and this is just the beginning. However, looking back and appreciating what God has done is essential. As a minister, Junior knows once said: "It is possible to limit God," it says in Psalms, 78:41-42 KJV "Yea, they turned back and tempted God, and limited the Holy One of Israel. They remembered not his hand, nor the day when he delivered them from the enemy."

They limited God in their current situation because they could not remember what He had done for them, where He had taken them from, and His deliverance. Let us always remember how good God is. Take every opportunity to exalt His Holy name and to serve Him. Ephesians 5: 16 "Redeeming the time, because the days are evil," another translation says, "making the most of every opportunity because the days are evil." Let's take every opportunity to speak to God. To that end, if you don't know Jesus as your personal saviour and want to get to know him, please consider this prayer.

In the words of Billy Graham (paraphrased):

"Dear, Lord Jesus, I know that I am a sinner, and I ask for Your forgiveness. I believe You died, and Your blood was shed for my sins, and You rose from the dead. I repent from my sins and invite You to come into my heart and life. I want to trust and follow You as my Lord and Savior. In Your Name. Amen.

Revelation 12:11 — "And they overcame him by the blood of the Lamb, and by the word of their testimony, and they loved not their lives unto the death."

Remember that you are an overcomer.

NOTE TO READER

Dear, Reader

Thank you for taking the time to navigate Junior's journey with me. I am delighted to let you know that from the lessons strewn throughout the book I have created a perfect workbook as a tool to help us apply these lessons to our lives and enable us to also discover our own unique imprint and journey.

Please visit Amazon and all other bookseller platforms for your copy. Do not hesitate to share your experience with your friends and network, and by way of reviews on any platform you ordered your copy from.

If you would like to connect with me personally or want me to share with your group or at an event, please reach out to me directly via email: don.e.scott84@gmail.com

Watch out for Part II. Until then I wish you the very best in all you do.

Thank you!

God bless you!

www.ingramcontent.com/pod-product-compliance
Lightning Source LLC
Chambersburg PA
CBHW051728050726
47598CB00003B/1090